Janet Jackson

Janet Jackson

by D. L. Mabery

Lerner Publications Company
Minneapolis

LIBRARY OF CONGRESS CATALOGING-IN-PUBLICATION DATA

Mabery, D. L.
  Janet Jackson/D. L. Mabery.
      p.   cm.
  Summary: A biography of Janet Jackson, "baby" in a famous family,
who is not only Michael Jackson's sister, but a strong singing
talent who has also worked in television.
  ISBN 0-8225-1618-7
  1. Jackson, Janet, 1966-   —Juvenile literature. 2. Singers—
United States—Biography—Juvenile literature. [1. Jackson,
Janet, 1966-   2. Singers.   3. Afro-Americans—Biography.]
I. Title.
ML3930.J15M3 1988
784.5′4′00924—dc19
[B]
[920]
                                                       88-2704
                                                         CIP
                                                       AC MN

        3   4   5   6   7   8   9   10   98   97   96   95   94   93   92   91

Contents

Woman in Control

Janet Jackson's life story is a story about control, as she says in the brief spoken message at the beginning of her hit album *Control*: "Control of what I say, control of what I do. And this time I'm going to do it my way."

The lyrics of "Control" express how Janet felt in 1986, the year she recorded that song. She always did what people told her, she sings. But she's learned a lot about herself and what she can accomplish, and she is putting that education to use by taking control of her actions.

"All my life I've had to please others," she said at the time *Control* was released. "Now I'm going to make myself happy."

Control is more than a hit album that produced six chart-topping singles. It's the record that established Janet Jackson, the "baby" of one of the most famous families in show business, as a star in her own right. The album made people realize that Janet is not just Michael Jackson's sister, but a woman with strong singing talents of her own.

Before she could become a success, though, Janet herself had to realize how talented she was and that she could make it on her own. And *Control* is the album with which Janet Jackson declared her independence.

"I'm really excited," she said in 1986. That year *Control*'s nine songs seemed to be played on every radio station and in every dance club, while Janet's videos constantly played on MTV, the television station that shows music videos. "I knew *Control* was good, but I didn't think it would take off like it has."

People who knew Janet, however, always thought she had what it took to be a major star. In fact, her older brother Michael told her years ago that she could be as successful as she wanted to be. "He said I didn't realize how talented I am," Janet remembered later.

Three years before *Control* was recorded, one of the executives at A & M Records, Janet Jackson's record company, predicted that it would only be a matter of time before she became a star. "She's shy, but as soon as she starts singing, she lights up," he said. "You can't help but fall in love with her. There's another lady inside Janet who's getting ready to come out."

The "other lady" who came out on the *Control* album was a confident, smart young woman who no longer worried about her looks or about pleasing other people. That woman had learned a lot about herself.

An Entertaining Family

It is no surprise that Janet Jackson became a singer. Music was an important part of the Jackson household while she was growing up. Before she was born, her father, Joe, played guitar for a band called the Falcons. But as the Jackson family grew larger, Joe had to quit the band to work as a crane operator in the steel mills of Gary, Indiana. Since there wasn't much money left after paying the bills to buy toys for the Jackson kids, Katherine, Janet's mother, taught them to sing.

11

"In Gary, kids don't have anything to do except go to school and come home," Mrs. Jackson said.

By the time Janet Damita Jackson was born, on May 16, 1966, her oldest sister, Maureen, was already married and living away from home. Janet was the youngest of nine children. By the time she was three years old, her five oldest brothers—Jackie, Tito, Jermaine, Marlon, and Michael—had formed a singing group. The boys spent most of their free time after school rehearsing.

Joe Jackson was proud of his sons' singing abilities, and he helped them practice by teaching them new songs. The Jackson Five, as they called themselves, began winning talent shows in and around Gary, and the living room of the Jacksons' house at 825 Jackson Street was soon filled with trophies.

The group came to the attention of Berry Gordy, the head of Motown Records, and the Jackson Five signed a recording contract with Gordy. The group's first single, "I Want You Back," was released in the fall of 1969 and went straight to the top of the record charts. Many other hit records followed, and the Jackson family moved into a Tudor-style mansion near Los Angeles, where Motown Records was located.

"I never really played with neighborhood kids..." Janet remembered, "but that never bothered me." Instead, she stayed around home, playing with the small zoo of animals the family owns. The Jacksons have swans, parrots, deer, a peacock, a snake, and a llama. (Llamas come from South America and are related to camels, but llamas are smaller and do not have a hump.)

Janet (front) was just 11 years old when her family's television show, "The Jacksons," premiered. Other family members are: center (left to right), Randy, LaToya, Rebbie; rear (left to right), Jackie, Michael, Tito, and Marlon.

When Janet was seven years old, she appeared on stage for the first time. The Jackson Five was giving a concert at the MGM Grand Hotel in Las Vegas, Nevada. Janet mimicked Mae West, a sassy actress from the early days of movies. Two years later, on a Jackson family television show, Janet again performed her comic mimicry of Mae West, as well as of singer Cher.

Television producer Norman Lear saw Janet on the television special and asked her to try out for a part on one of his television comedy shows. The show, "Good Times," was about a black family living in a Chicago housing project. At the age of 10, Janet was cast as Penny Gordon Woods, a physically abused girl. Janet played Penny through 1979, when "Good Times" went off the air.

"The cast made me feel so welcome that it became my second family," Janet said.

Early in 1981, when Janet was 14, she got another acting job. This time she played Charlene DuPrey, the girlfriend of Willis on the comedy "Diff'rent Strokes." Describing the character of Charlene, Janet said, "She's a shy girl, somewhat like me, who says what she feels."

Her brothers' singing group — which was now called The Jacksons and included Randy, the youngest brother —was still recording best-selling albums. Michael, in particular, was well on his way to becoming a world-wide singing superstar.

But between acting and school, Janet was too busy to think about singing.

"It's hard sometimes to manage your career and school

Janet played Penny Gordon Woods on "Good Times" with Jimmie Walker.

because you have to worry about your grades all the time," she said while she was working on "Diff'rent Strokes." Because television studios want child actors to do well in school, the kids must make good grades in order to stay on the show. "If you get below a 'C' you can't work," Janet said.

In 1982, however, Janet followed her brothers into the world of music when she recorded and released her first album, titled simply *Janet Jackson*. The album stayed on the rhythm and blues charts for almost a year. It contained three hit singles, including a song called "Young Love." Still, Janet wasn't thrilled by the experience.

"On my first album, the songs were sort of teen-age like," she told *Jet* magazine in 1984. "I wanted to make a change for my second album. The first album introduces you. The second one sets your image." She worried that if she didn't change her sound on her second album, people would always think of her as a little girl.

All the same, recording her first album had a positive effect on the youngest member of the Jackson family. Because none of her famous brothers had helped her with that album, Janet realized that she could do something on her own.

"People didn't buy it because Michael sang background or wrote or produced," she said about her first album. That achievement was a turning point in her life, giving her a first taste of musical independence. "I'd like to get my own sound, go in a totally different direction from my brothers," she stated after the *Janet Jackson* album came out.

Janet had good reason to be concerned about what the public might think of her singing career. It would be easy for people to believe that the only reason Janet could make a record was because her brothers, especially Michael, were famous.

Michael had always been the Jackson Five's lead singer and focal point. By the time Janet's first album was released, Michael had become one of the biggest-selling artists in the recording industry. In 1972, when he was

16

14 years old, he released "Ben," a single he recorded without his brothers. The record sold more copies than any other Motown release in 10 years.

Seven years later, Michael released a solo album called *Off the Wall*. The record went to Number Three on the charts, contained four Top Ten singles, and sold more than five million copies. Then, in late 1982, Michael's *Thriller* album was released. *Thriller* has become the biggest-selling album in the history of recorded music. It has sold over 38 million copies.

In 1984, while Michael's *Thriller* was still high in the charts, Janet's second album, *Dream Street*, was released. During this time, Janet continued to work as an actress, appearing regularly on the television series "Fame" and making a guest appearance on "The Love Boat."

Even though it seemed that Michael's recording success would overshadow Janet's, the brother and sister don't compete. "As long as one of us is at the top, that makes the rest of us happy," Janet said.

Janet and Michael have always been close. "He gave me books to read," Janet remembered. "When I finished a book, he'd say, 'OK, you should read this one.'" And when Michael was away on tour, he'd always send Janet presents. "Out of everyone in our family, Michael and I are the most alike," she said.

In 1984, while Michael and her other brothers were touring the world and performing the songs from *Thriller*, Janet took another step toward independence. She ran off and got married.

Going to the Chapel

Janet Jackson and singer James DeBarge had been friends since she was 10 years old. Like the Jackson family, the DeBarges had also formed a singing group. El, Randy, Mark, James, and their sister Bunny had struck gold with their second album, *All This Love*. Like the Jacksons, the DeBarge family played rhythm and blues music, which made their records popular in the dance clubs.

On Labor Day in 1984, when Janet was 18, she and

James went to Grand Rapids, Michigan—James's hometown—and got married. Neither one of them had told their parents about what they were planning.

"I didn't tell anybody when I did it, but my sister LaToya," Janet remembered. "I just up and did it."

In fact, the news of her marriage got home before she did: her parents read about the wedding in the newspaper. Even though 18 seems like a young age to get married, Janet was carrying on a family tradition. Her parents, Joe and Katherine, married young, as did her brothers Jackie, Tito, Jermaine, and Marlon. So Joe wished Janet and James the best of luck, and Katherine opened her arms to the newlyweds.

Janet's marriage didn't even last a year, however. What went wrong? Janet blames her and James's separate and demanding work schedules. Janet was working on the television show "Fame" at the time, and James was busy recording with his brothers and sisters.

"He would be in the studio all night until maybe 2:30 A.M. or 3:00 A.M.," Janet said, "and I would have to get up at 4:00 A.M. to be on the 'Fame' set." Even though the marriage didn't work out, Janet said she is still good friends with James, and she doesn't believe that 18 is too young to get married.

"It was a really great experience and I learned a lot from it," she said. Part of her lesson was recognizing the demands of marriage. "Marriage is a big responsibility and requires a lot of time that James and I both need to spend on our careers," she said.

Single again, Janet devotes her time to her career.

Out on Her Own

After leaving "Fame" in 1985, Janet decided to devote her time and energy to a singing career. "I'm more serious about my career than I have ever been," Janet said shortly after *Control* came out. "I'm just taking control of my life and I'm more serious about my work. That's what the album is all about—control—and doing what I want to do."

Before she got to that point, however, she had to do a few things that she didn't really want to do. One was to leave her home in Los Angeles and spend three months by herself in Minneapolis, Minnesota, rehearsing and recording material for a new album.

A & M Records executive John McClain asked Janet to attend dance classes and go on a diet to lose some weight. He also hooked her up with two of the hottest producers in the record industry, James "Jimmy Jam" Harris III and Terry Lewis. The pair had written and produced a number of Top Ten hits by the time Janet entered their studio.

Jimmy and Terry requested that Janet come to their Minneapolis studio by herself. "We felt it was important to get her out of the protective, fairy-tale life she had been leading," Jimmy Jam said. For example, out in California, Janet never had to drive a car, even though she was old enough to drive. She always had someone to drive for her. In Minneapolis, Jimmy loaned his car to Janet and told her she'd have to drive it herself.

Jimmy Jam and Terry also interviewed Janet and took notes about her life. They wanted to get to know her so they could write songs that spoke about her life. They try to bring out the personalities of the artists they work with.

"We knew we could do something with her," Jimmy Jam said about Janet after meeting her. "But she needed to get away from everything so she could let herself go. She was a bomb getting ready to explode. All she needed was the right fuse."

Jimmy Jam and Terry Lewis got their start in music as members of a band called The Time, which was produced by Prince. By 1982, around the time of Michael Jackson's rise to superstardom and Janet's first recording experience, Terry and Jimmy Jam were beginning to produce songs for other artists. They had to leave The Time because producing songs took up more and more of their energies.

As producers, Harris and Lewis help shape the sounds of a record by knowing what instruments to use, when to add backing vocals, and how loud or soft to record various musical passages.

On Janet's first two records, the instrumental tracks had been completed before she got to the studio. All she had to do was learn the lyrics and sing into a microphone.

For her third album, she wanted to do things differently. "This time around, I intended to be completely involved in the recording process, from the songwriting to the playing to the production," she said. And she was: Janet helped Terry and Jimmy Jam write all but two of the songs on the album. She also played keyboards and co-produced the album.

Control was released in September 1985. The album has an upbeat, disco sound. The songs, which Janet says express how she felt at the time, deal with love, loss, and assertiveness. With the help of the energetic dance videos for her songs "What Have You Done for Me Lately?" and "Nasty," the album became a Number One hit.

When the album came out, it surprised a lot of her fans. "Everyone perceived me as being little and

When she sings, Janet expresses many feelings, such as love, loss, and assertiveness.

innocent," she said. "I'm not saying that I'm devilish, but I'm not an angel either."

"Janet is carving her own little niche in the history of that family," Jimmy Jam said. The album got a lot of the rebelliousness out of Janet, he thought.

Six of *Control*'s singles became Number One hits on the rhythm and blues charts, beating a previous record set by her brother Michael's *Thriller* album. Because *Control* became a Number One album on the pop charts, Janet and Michael became the first brother and sister ever to have Number One albums.

Staying in Control

Even though Janet Jackson had taken control of her singing career and was considered a star in the music world, she had something else to prove to herself.

On her follow-up to *Control,* Janet again tackled new musical challenges. But the songs on the album called *Rhythm Nation 1814* also take on social problems such as homelessness, illiteracy, bigotry, drugs, and violence.

"We have so little time to solve these problems," Janet explained. "I want people to realize the urgency. I want to grab their attention. Music is my way of doing that."

Rhythm Nation certainly attracted attention. The 1989 album, also produced by Jimmy Jam and Terry Lewis, sold over two million copies in less than five weeks. And critics and fans noticed a new, grown-up Janet who was not afraid to take a stand on important issues.

The latest star in a family of stars, Janet takes to her fame quite naturally, although she's careful not to get lost in the shuffle. Even though her brothers helped her with *Dream Street*, her second album, she isn't sure if she'll use their services in the future. After all, she feels, it took her long enough to establish an identity separate from the Jackson Five.

Janet said she has learned a lot about being on her own, and she is grateful for the help she's received from her producers and friends. "It helps...for people to give you encouragement and to let you know that you can succeed and to keep pushing you. I have so much more confidence in myself than I ever did before."

That confidence has put Janet Jackson on the top—and in control.

Janet grew up in the family mansion in the San Fernando Valley
near Los Angeles, California.

Janet's mother, Katherine Jackson, taught her children to sing when they were growing up.

Photo Credits:

Paul Lovelace/Retna Ltd., p. 1
Ron Wolfson/London Features International, p. 2
Julian Barton/Retna Ltd., p. 6
Phototeque, pp. 10, 13, 15
Ralph Dominguez/Globe Photos, p. 18
Chris Walter/Retna Ltd., pp. 21, 28
Doug Vann/Globe Photos, p. 22
John Bellissimo/Retna Ltd., p. 26
Photo Features International, p. 31
AP/Wide World Photos, p. 32

Front and back cover photos by John Bellissimo/Retna Ltd.

DATE DUE

SEP 17 '97			
MAY 14 '99			
MAY 21 '99			
AP 03 '00			
AP 20 '00			
DEC 19 '03			
GAYLORD			PRINTED IN U.S.A.